a water bed

I'm writting

in curseve

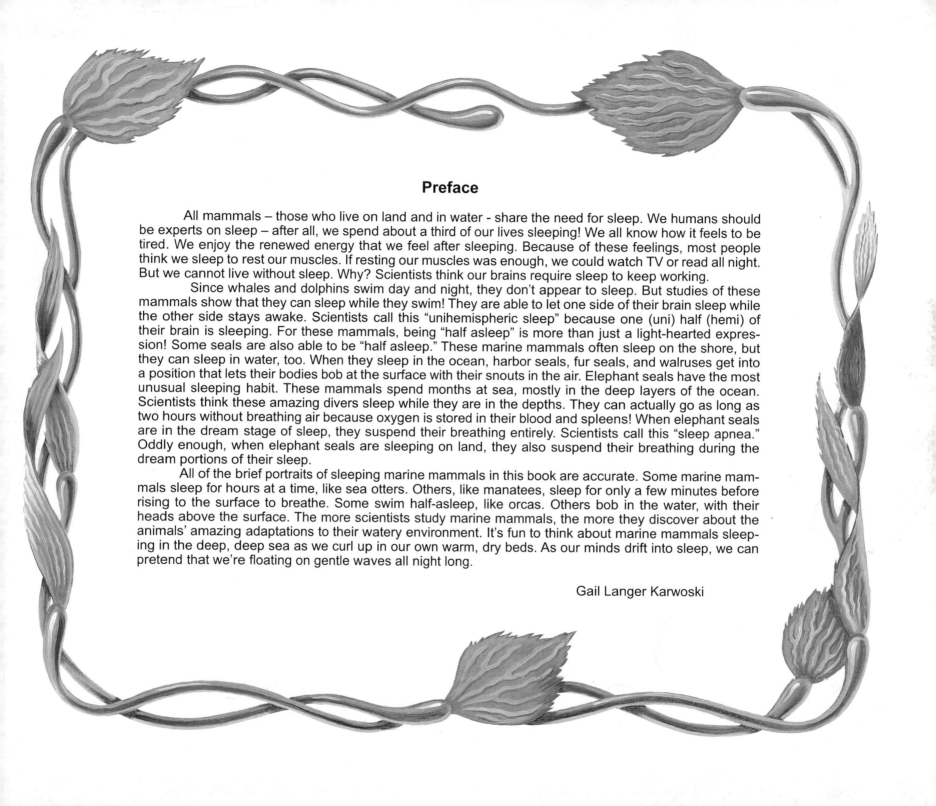

Preface

All mammals – those who live on land and in water - share the need for sleep. We humans should be experts on sleep – after all, we spend about a third of our lives sleeping! We all know how it feels to be tired. We enjoy the renewed energy that we feel after sleeping. Because of these feelings, most people think we sleep to rest our muscles. If resting our muscles was enough, we could watch TV or read all night. But we cannot live without sleep. Why? Scientists think our brains require sleep to keep working.

Since whales and dolphins swim day and night, they don't appear to sleep. But studies of these mammals show that they can sleep while they swim! They are able to let one side of their brain sleep while the other side stays awake. Scientists call this "unihemispheric sleep" because one (uni) half (hemi) of their brain is sleeping. For these mammals, being "half asleep" is more than just a light-hearted expression! Some seals are also able to be "half asleep." These marine mammals often sleep on the shore, but they can sleep in water, too. When they sleep in the ocean, harbor seals, fur seals, and walruses get into a position that lets their bodies bob at the surface with their snouts in the air. Elephant seals have the most unusual sleeping habit. These mammals spend months at sea, mostly in the deep layers of the ocean. Scientists think these amazing divers sleep while they are in the depths. They can actually go as long as two hours without breathing air because oxygen is stored in their blood and spleens! When elephant seals are in the dream stage of sleep, they suspend their breathing entirely. Scientists call this "sleep apnea." Oddly enough, when elephant seals are sleeping on land, they also suspend their breathing during the dream portions of their sleep.

All of the brief portraits of sleeping marine mammals in this book are accurate. Some marine mammals sleep for hours at a time, like sea otters. Others, like manatees, sleep for only a few minutes before rising to the surface to breathe. Some swim half-asleep, like orcas. Others bob in the water, with their heads above the surface. The more scientists study marine mammals, the more they discover about the animals' amazing adaptations to their watery environment. It's fun to think about marine mammals sleeping in the deep, deep sea as we curl up in our own warm, dry beds. As our minds drift into sleep, we can pretend that we're floating on gentle waves all night long.

Gail Langer Karwoski

I have been gathering information for this book for over six years, and I have many people to thank. In addition to collecting information from published books and articles, I've talked with people who work with marine mammals at several major aquariums. Three were particularly generous with their time and knowledge: Nedra Hecker, former Curator of Marine Mammals at the National Aquarium in Baltimore, Maryland; Mary Church, Educator at Sea World in Orlando, Florida; and Jenny Montague, Assistant Curator of Marine Mammals at the New England Aquarium in Boston, Massachusetts.

My husband and first reader, Chester Karwoski, helped me capture complex ideas in simple language. The "Four at Five" writers group – Loretta Hammer, Wanda Langley, and Bettye Stroud – also contributed suggestions.

To my "soul sister," Marilyn Gootman – a continuing source of
inspiration about friendship, parenting, and now...grand-parenting!
Many thanks to all ... and to all a good sleep. – Gail Langer Karwoski

To Geoff and Thomas – Connie McLennan

Library of Congress Control Number: 2005921090
A catalog record for this book is available from the Library of Congress.

Summary: A soothing bedtime story that shows how marine mammals breathe while they sleep in the ocean.
Tuck into some kelp little otter. Close one eye, baby dolphin. Float like a cloud, baby beluga. Pleasant dreams young child.

ISBN: 0-9764943-1-0

Juvenile Fiction/Bedtime & Dreams
Juvenile Fiction/Animals/Marine Life
Juvenile Fiction/Animals/Mammals
Juvenile Nonfiction/Nature/Water (Oceans, Lakes, etc.)
Juvenile Nonfiction/Animals Marine Life

Sylvan Dell Publishing
976 Houston Northcutt Blvd., Suite 3
Mt. Pleasant, SC 29464

www.SylvanDellPublishing.com

Water Beds

Sleeping in the Ocean

By Gail Langer Karwoski   Illustrated by Connie McLennan

I love killer Whales, baby.

It's night, little person, and you're tucked in your warm, dry bed. Have you ever wondered what it would be like to sleep in the deep, deep sea?

good night

Orcas sleep as they glide side-by-side in their pod. Four minutes of rest, then up to breathe. Up they come, one after another - a rhythmic dance of black and white in the blue sea.

Harbor seals may haul out on the shore or hover in the sea. With flippers tucked against their sides, they hang like bottles in the water. Only their slick foreheads, closed eyes, and whiskered snouts poke above the surface.

Dolphins nap half-asleep - one eye closed to rest, one eye open to watch. A sleep in the deep can be dangerous, so wide-awake dolphins swim 'round the sleepyheads and keep them safe.

Manatees sleep in warm rivers and in the sea. They rest both snout and tail on sandy riverbeds. Every few minutes, they rise like bubbles to the surface and breathe. Slowly they sink to snooze again.

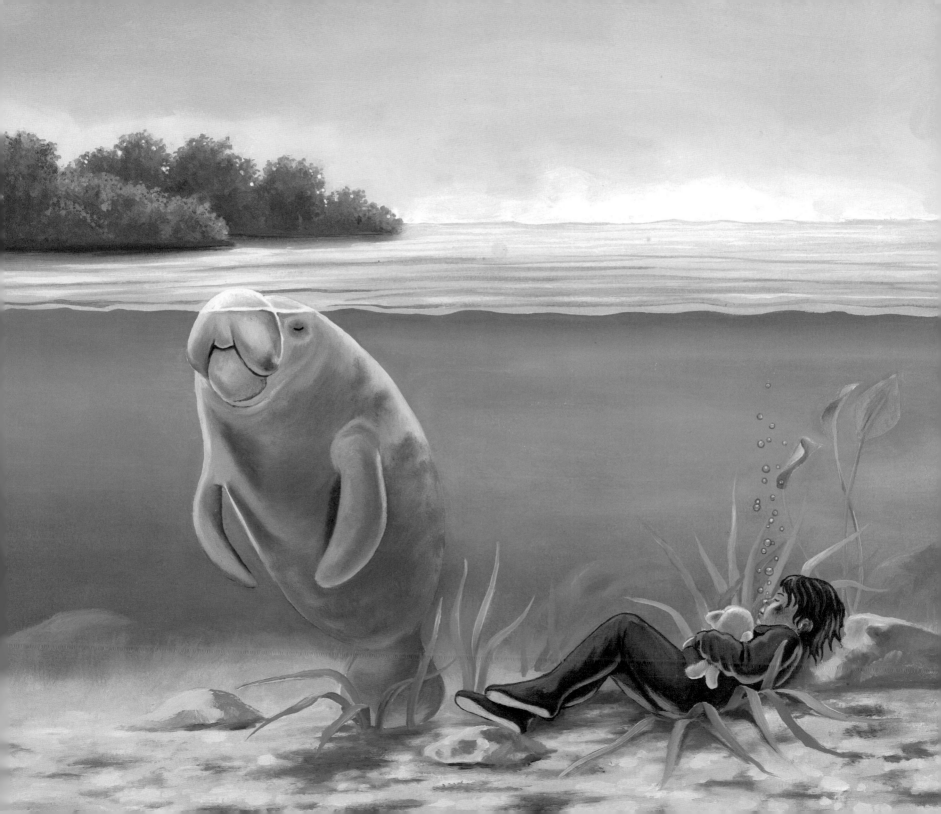

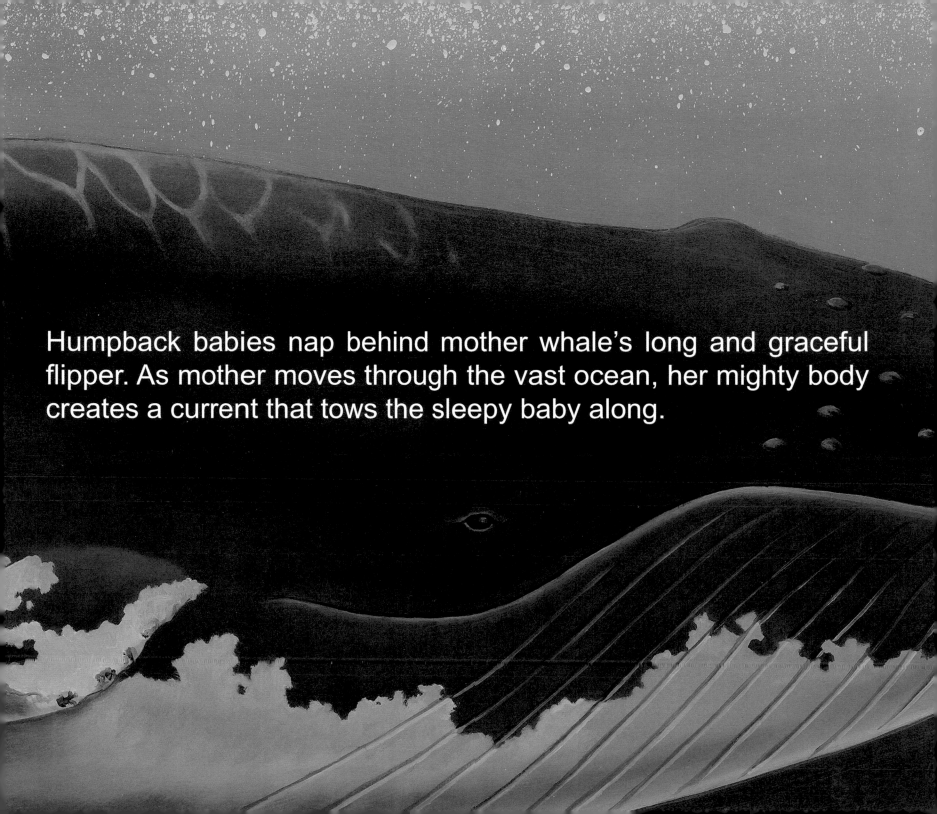

Humpback babies nap behind mother whale's long and graceful flipper. As mother moves through the vast ocean, her mighty body creates a current that tows the sleepy baby along.

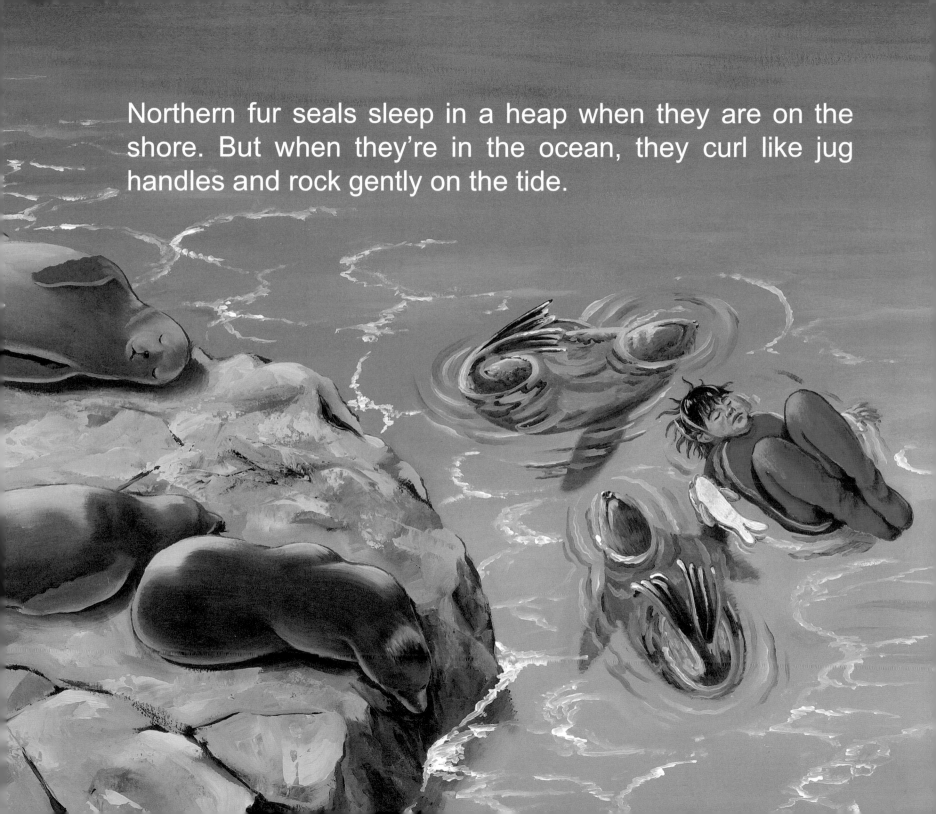

Northern fur seals sleep in a heap when they are on the shore. But when they're in the ocean, they curl like jug handles and rock gently on the tide.

Beluga whales float like white clouds, their blowholes in the air. Or they doze peacefully beneath rich, northern waters.

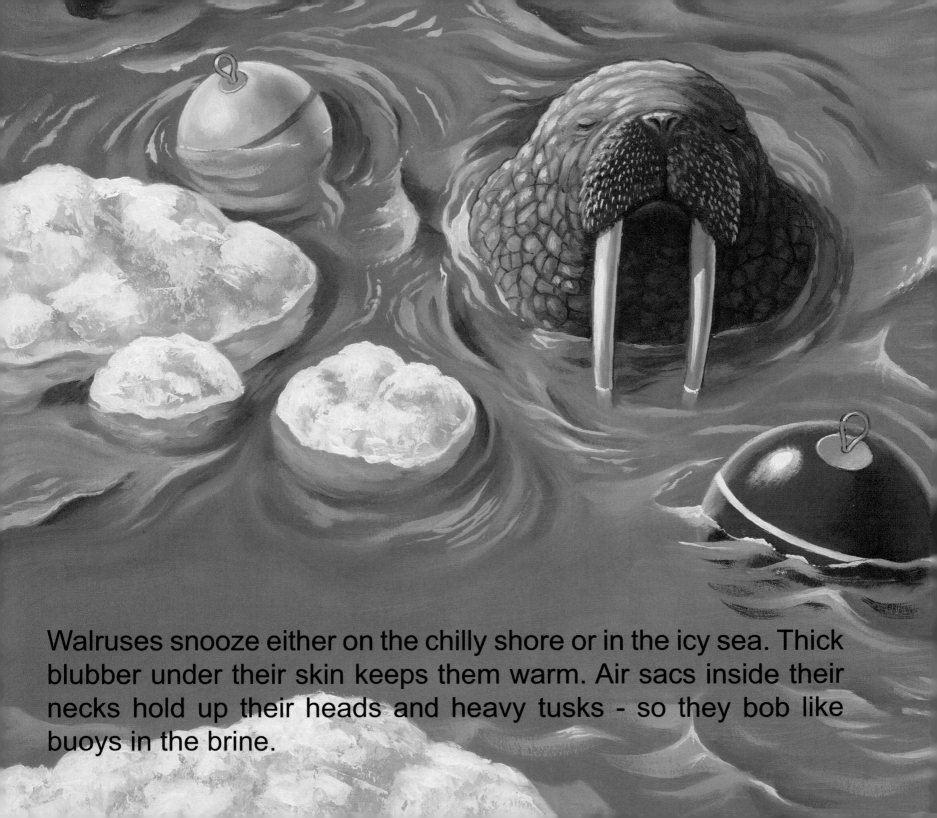

Walruses snooze either on the chilly shore or in the icy sea. Thick blubber under their skin keeps them warm. Air sacs inside their necks hold up their heads and heavy tusks - so they bob like buoys in the brine.

Elephant seals pop through the surface to breathe in and out. Down, down, down they dive through dark, deep water. Far below danger, they dream undisturbed.

Sea otters doze above undersea kelp forests, wrapping the kelp strands around their tummies to anchor themselves in place. When it's very cold, they blanket their faces with furry front paws. Then they shut their eyes tight and sleep through the night.

It's fun to imagine a sleep in the deep, but a warm, cozy bed is the perfect spot for you to sleep. Open your mouth and give a great big yawn - you won't swallow a drop of salty water! Curl up, little person. Stretch out and sink onto your soft pillow. As you drift into deep blue dreams, you will float on gentle waves all night long.

For Creative Minds

What makes an animal a mammal? Mammals share certain characteristics. All mammals are warm-blooded and breathe air. They have hair and large brains. All mammals protect their young and feed their babies on mother's milk. There are about 4,000 types of mammals. Most mammals live on land. People are one type of mammal. Cats and dogs are mammals. So are many farm animals, such as cows, goats, and horses. Zoo animals - like monkeys, kangaroos, and hippos - are mammals. Bats are mammals that can fly. Marine mammals are mammals that live in or depend on the ocean.

Scientists sort marine mammals into three groups, or *orders*. One is called the *cetaceans* and includes all the whales and dolphins. Another is called the *carnivora* and includes polar bears, sea otters, and the *pinnipeds* - seals, sea lions, and walruses. A third is called *sirenians* and includes manatees and their relatives, the dugongs.

Marine mammals have special adaptations so they can live in the ocean:

- Marine mammals are able to store oxygen longer than land mammals, so they can stay underwater for longer periods.

- Whales and walruses have a thick layer of blubber under their skin to keep them warm in cold waters.

- A blowhole at the top of the head helps dolphins and whales to breathe easily while swimming. They can keep their heads underwater to watch for predators or food while they breathe! Some cetaceans have one blowhole while others have two.

- Nostrils stay closed when marine mammals swim.

- Dolphins' and whales' tails (called flukes) move up and down to help them swim. They use their front flippers to steer.

- Eared seals (sea lions and fur seals) use their front flippers for swimming. Non-eared seals use their back flippers for swimming.

- Seals have claws on their front flippers but mostly move on land by rolling on their bellies. Sea lions & fur seals use their hind flippers to "walk" on land.

- Walruses use their tusks to help pull themselves ashore.

- Manatees use their paddle-like front flippers for swimming or "walking" along on the ground. Sometimes they even use their flippers to hold things and to bring food to their mouths! (Manatees can live in fresh and salt water and only eat plants – they love their greens!)

Make Your Own Marine Mammal Using Adaptations

Trace, copy, or download line art at www.SylvanDellPublishing.com – click on "Water Beds." Select the adaptations you want your animal to have, then cut out, color, and tape or glue to the "body." There are choices from each of the three orders. The examples on the next page will show you what a real marine animal looks like. When you are finished mixing and matching body parts for your special animal, give your animal a name, describe how it will live, eat, swim, and, of course, sleep.

1) Select the shape of the body. All bodies are smooth and streamlined for ease of swimming.

2) Select the shape of the head and attach it to the body.

3) Will your animal breathe through a nose or blowhole? Draw the nose or blowhole(s) on the head.

4) Draw eyes on the head where you think they should go. Large eyes help animals to see in the dark water. Eyes closer to the top of the head are good for animals that like to float with their head above water. Eyes further down on the side of the head make it easier for animals with blowholes to see in the water when they come up for breath.

5) Will your animal live in warm or cold water? If it lives in cold water, how will it stay warm – fur or blubber? Blubber is a heavy layer of fat that helps to keep marine mammals warm in cold water. Draw fur onto the body if the animal has fur.

6) How will your animal swim – flippers or flukes? Pick out a pair of front flippers and either back flippers or flukes (tail). If your animal will have a dorsal fin (on top of its "back") to help stabilize it as it swims, add it now.

7) Will your marine mammal be able to climb onto land? If so, will it have claws on the front flippers? Draw onto the animal.

8) Sea lions, fur seals, and sea otters have external ear flaps – like us. Cetaceans "hear" by using echolocation (they send out a sound that bounces back to tell the cetacean where something is). How will your animal hear? Draw ears if desired.

9) How and what will your animal eat? If your animal eats plankton, it will have baleen. Animals with teeth can eat fish and other animals or plants.

10) Some marine mammals (pinnipeds) use "whiskers" to find food. The walrus uses its tusks to dig for food in the sand. Draw whiskers or tusks if desired.

All marine mammals have special adaptations so they do not need to breathe as often as land mammals. They also have adaptations that enable them to dive deep for food.

For Bibliography information, please go to www.SylvanDellPublishing.com and click on the "Water Beds" page.

Heads & Mouths

Dorsal Fins

Front Flippers

Flukes and Rear Flippers

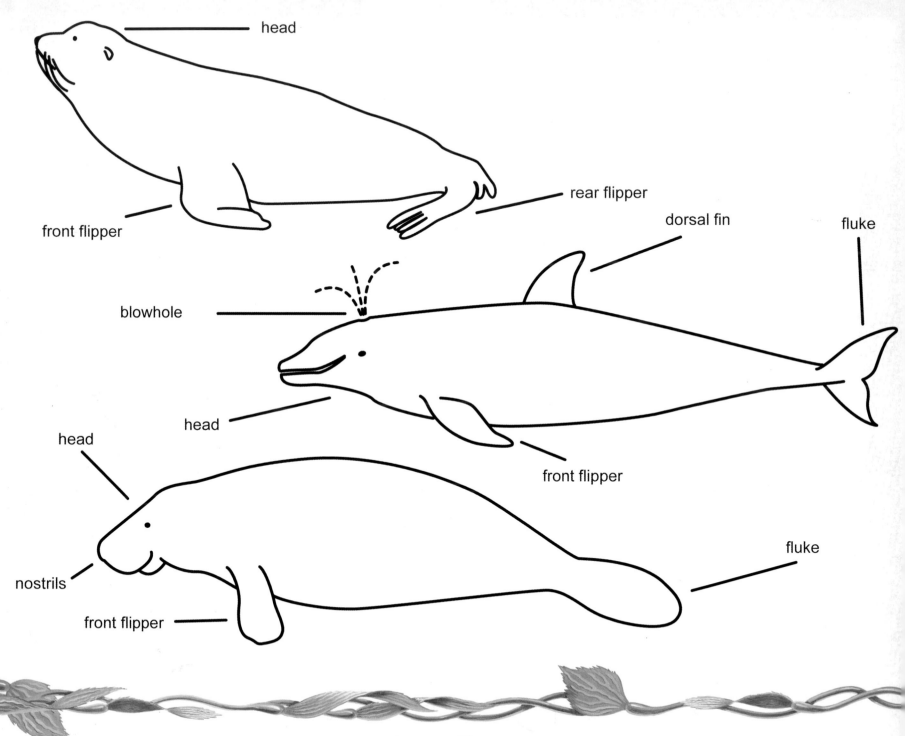

head

front flipper

rear flipper

dorsal fin

fluke

blowhole

head

head

front flipper

nostrils

front flipper

fluke